JOHN WORSLEY

The illustrations by John Worsley in the *Purnell Colour Classics* series have greatly added to the impact and charm of these dramatic stories. Now well established as a portrait painter and marine artist, John Worsley was in the navy during the war. Taken prisoner, he and a fellow officer constructed an astonishingly life-like dummy to help in their escape plan. After the war he was appointed adviser to the makers of the famous war film, *Albert RN*, which tells the true story of this remarkable feat.

Published 1979 by Purnell Books,
Berkshire House, Queen Street, Maidenhead, Berkshire.

Designed and produced for Purnell Books by
Intercontinental Book Productions.

Printed by Purnell & Sons Ltd, Paulton (Bristol) and London.

SBN 361 04402 X

R. D. Blackmore's

Lorna Doone

Retold by Jane Carruth

Purnell

A sad homecoming

If anybody cares to read a simple tale told simply, I John Ridd, of the parish of Oare in the county of Somerset, will now try to set it down in order, God sparing my life and memory.

Of my time at that worthy grammar school in Tiverton in Devon to which my father sent me for my education, I will say nothing – for my story most truly begins on the day John Fry, my father's man, appeared at the school to fetch me home. It was the day when I was twelve years old, the 29th of November, 1673.

"Why hasn't Father come himself to fetch me?" I demanded. "He always comes himself."

But John, who had ridden all the way from Oare to Tiverton, a long and painful journey, seemed more concerned to rest not only himself, but also his nag Smiler, and my own pony Peggy, which would carry me home. No matter how I questioned him he would not give me a straight answer about my father and I was all at once overcome by a sense of foreboding.

We set out early the next morning, my wardrobe strapped on Smiler's back, and reached the town of Dulverton at noon.

John took me to a hostel and ordered an excellent meal of mutton pasty. It was a thing I had often heard of from very wealthy boys and men, and to hear them talk of it made my lips smack. Now I sampled it and was not disappointed.

Afterwards I went out to the pump to wash. While I was running the water off my head and shoulders, a dark-skinned, foreign, lady's maid came out and asked me to pump the water for her. This I did until the long Italian glass which she held out was filled with clear water. Whereupon she smiled at me and made some flattering remark about my blue eyes.

As we left Dulverton town and began climbing the steep hill, we came upon a great coach and six horses labouring very heavily. In the front seat of the crimson coach, I saw the foreign woman I had met at the pump and, beside her, a dark-haired little girl, very richly attired. In

the back seat, opposite these two, there was a fine lady, warmly dressed, with a small boy of two or three, who had a white cockade in his hat.

I took off my cap to the grand lady, who was very beautiful, and she kissed her hand to me, whereupon I was so startled by this courtesy that I dug my heels into Peggy and she broke away and bore me rapidly up the hill.

We saw no more of the coach, for presently we turned off the road on to the moors. Soon the fog came down as thick as ever I saw it, and after awhile it was almost too dark to see anything except shadowy patches in the dusk, as the fading light crept up the valleys.

"Mercy of God! Where be us now?" John Fry asked.

And I answered that I had no idea.

We drew our horses up and listened, and then John, whose brave red beard I could no longer make out, so dark it was, shook his bridle-arm, and smote Smiler merrily. He had suddenly heard the mournful swinging of the gibbet chains.

"Us be near the Doone-track now," he whispered, "two mile from Dunkery Beacon Hill."

I knew Dunkery Beacon Hill was the highest place on Exmoor and the haunt of the dreaded outlaws, the Doones of Bagworthy. They were the awe of all Devon and Somerset, and my legs began to tremble to and fro upon Peggy's sides as I thought of these traitors and murderers.

We rode very cautiously now down the slope and were just facing the next hill when there came the sound of horses' feet, the grunting of weary men, and occasionally the clank of iron mixed with the wheezy groaning of leather.

"For God's sake, Jack, slip round her belly, and let her go where she wull," John Fry whispered, and I obeyed.

Just as the foremost horseman passed, scarce twenty yards below us, a puff of wind came up the glen, and the fog rolled away. All at once a strong red light spread like fingers over the moorland and lit up the steel of the riders.

"Dunkery Beacon!" John hissed in my ear. "Fired to show the Doones the way home . . ."

I wriggled away from his restraining arm until I was under a grey patch of stone, fringed with dry fern and scarce twenty feet above the heads of the riders. They passed by me in silence and I saw how big and heavy they were and how

recklessly they carried their guns. They wore leathern jerkins, and long boots, and iron plates on their breasts and heads, and there were more than thirty of them. One had a child flung across his saddlebow. It was very young and my heart grieved for it, but whether it was alive or dead it was impossible to tell.

I was so roused at the sight of the poor little thing that I forgot my fear of the Doones and stood up and shouted at them. One turned in the saddle as if he had it in mind to take a shot at me. But another shouted that I was nothing more than a pixie and best left alone.

After they had gone we rode homewards and even when we were at the gates of the farm itself my father was not there. Nor would he ever be, for, as I was soon to learn, he had been cruelly murdered – killed by the Doones of Bagworthy, while riding home from market.

Now I understood why John Fry had kept silent about my father, and why he could not bear to tell me the bitter truth.

Thus it was that I found myself head of the family, and the only man of it. I had no brothers, only two sisters – sweet-tempered, pretty Annie, two years younger than myself, and Eliza, sharp-tongued and very clever. And she was as yet too small to realize what it was to lose a father as good and kind and just as John Ridd of Plover's Barrows farm.

I meet Lorna for the first time

Almost everybody knows, in our part of the world at least, how pleasant and soft the fall of land is round our farm. All above it are the strong dark mountains, wild and desolate, but near our house the valleys are full of trees and bright green grass and scented orchards.

When I was about fourteen years old and still sadly missing my father, I resolved one day to explore the Bagworthy water and catch some loaches. There are many people, even now, who have no right knowledge of what a loach is and where he lives. I will not tell them, but there are few dishes my mother likes better than pickled loaches, and it was for her that I set out on the fishing expedition.

I never could forget how bitter cold the water was that Spring day. My shoes and

hose hung in a bag round my neck as I waded into the stream. In my hand I held a three-pronged fork firmly bound to a rod with a cord, and a piece of canvas kerchief, with a lump of bread inside it, and for more than a mile down the Lynn stream there was scarcely a stone that I left upturned. But it was as if all the loaches in the Lynn knew that I was come in search of them and were on the watch.

Then I took my courage in both hands and began venturing, where no grown man dared, up the Bagworthy water – though it must be confessed my heart beat faster at the very thought of the Doones and what they would do to me!

As I advanced I caught some very fine loaches. But now it was almost dusk, and the lonely desolate place where I found myself made me suddenly long for the comforts of our warm kitchen at home. I would not let myself turn back though, and presently I came to a great black pool flecked with foam-froth. I skirted round one side, at no little risk, for the rocks were high and steep. Then I came suddenly upon a waterfall, the sight of which made me suddenly draw in my breath.

It was then I slipped. I went down into that great black whirlpool, and might never have been heard of again if my trusty loach-fork had not stuck fast in the rock, and I was borne up upon it.

To my dismay and terror I saw that no choice was left me now except to climb up that hill of water or else be washed down back into the pool and whirled around till it drowned me. It would have been a difficult climb even without the slippery slime and the force of the river over it, and I had scant hope of ever gaining the summit. But then came the thought of my father and I gritted my teeth and began my course up the fearful torrent-way.

How long it was before I reached the top I have no idea, but at last the rush of

water, where first it came over the falls, drove me into the middle, and I stuck there for a while. I made one last effort to reach the top and then must have lost my senses, for when I came to again, my hands were full of young grass and a little girl was kneeling at my side.

As she rubbed my forehead tenderly with a dock leaf and a handkerchief, she whispered softly, "You will try to get better, won't you?"

Whereupon I sat upright, and my little saviour clapped her hands and asked my name, and what the big wet things were in the bag.

"My name is John Ridd," I told her, "and the bag is full of loaches for my mother. But I will give you some if you like. Now tell me your name."

"My name is Lorna Doone," she answered, in a low voice, as if ashamed of it. And she hung her pretty head and then burst into tears.

I comforted her in clumsy fashion for she looked like a royal princess as she sat there in her rich purple velvet dress. And though she was only a little girl, perhaps not more than eight years old, she had a strange dignity about her.

"When next I come, Lorna," I said, "I will bring you a puppy and some apples – only please give me your hand and do not weep so . . ."

Suddenly a shout came down the valley, and Lorna's face became terror-stricken. My heart began to beat violently and a tingle went through my bones, for I knew well what my fate would be if any of the murderous Doones discovered me.

Lorna pointed to a little niche in the rock which bordered the meadow.

"Look! Look!" She could hardly speak for terror. "There is a way out from the top of it. They would kill me if I told about it – oh, here they come . . ."

She turned as white as the snow which hung on the rocks above her, and I picked up my bag with the fishes in it and the three-pronged fork and drew her into a hiding place behind some bushes.

Crouching low beside her I saw a dozen fierce men come down, on the other side

of the water, not bearing guns, but joking and laughing as though out for a stroll.

"Queen! Queen!" some of them shouted. "Where are you? Where have you gone?"

"I know what I must do," I whispered. "I must get into the water, and you must go to sleep away in the meadow there."

She saw in a moment that this was the best thing to do, and she crept away. I crept into the water and lay down bodily in it, with my head between two blocks of stone, and some flood-drift combing over me. Dusk had deepened and there was a white mist over the river. Through it I glimpsed the little maid, pretending to be fast asleep under a rock. When the great rough men came round a corner and saw her they instantly stopped their shouting.

One of them caught her up in his arms, kissed her and roared, "Here she is! Here is our queen! Fast asleep, and unharmed!"

And he lifted her on his great square shoulder, and placed her narrow feet in one of his broad hands, and marched away with her, the rich purple velvet of her skirt ruffling the man's black beard.

When they were gone, I managed to crawl from the bank to the niche in the cliff, which Lorna had shown me, and felt myself going down some deep passage into a pit of darkness. With a chill and dread inside me which turned me into a coward, I reached the bottom. Then suddenly a robin sang in the brown fern and ivy behind me, and taking courage and comfort from its song, I scrambled back to the mouth of that pit as if the devil himself had been after me.

As I searched for a way out, the moon appeared over the edge of the mountain, and then I spied some rough steps, and rocky, made as if with a sledge-hammer. I began to climb, shivering with cold, and more than once was on the verge of giving up though I was bigger and stronger than any boy of my age. And when at last I was safely back at our farm nobody could get out of me how I had spent the day.

A celebrated highwayman

My mother's cousin, about whom she boasted in selected circles, was the famous highwayman Tom Faggus. He was a strongly built, merry gentleman whose every step was springy, although his legs were bowed with riding. To me he seemed very old but he was not much more than four-and-twenty.

He came one day to see us, riding his beautiful strawberry mare, Winnie. How I envied him that young spirited horse!

What a fool I was to imagine that such a filly would permit me to ride her! But there I was, as I met them in the yard, crying out that I could.

Annie laid hold of me as if I had been mad and Tom Faggus laughed, "There's none but me can do that, John."

But then in my foolishness I went on

arguing that I should be the second for there was no horse I could not ride. Suddenly Tom spoke very softly to the filly, who drew in her nostrils and and did all she could to answer him.

"Don't be too hard on him, sweetheart," said he. "Let him gently down on the mixen."

Then he turned the saddle off, and I was up in a moment. Winnie's master gave a shrill, clear whistle and I knew that I was in for it, for at the sound of the whistle she reared upright in the air; then finding me sticking to her still like wax, she took the courtyard gate at a leap, and then over the hedge, and away to the water-meadows. Where that gallop might have ended I dare not think, but there came at last another shrill whistle from the farm, and Winnie stopped as if with a bullet and set off for home with the speed of a swallow. I sat up again, but my strength was all spent, and as she rose at our gate, I tumbled off into the mixen!

My mother, who was the best in the world, scolded Tom for letting me risk my life on his mare. But Tom had a way with women and soon he was seated at our table eating the best she could provide. Annie hovered around and cast him many a shy glance.

We all knew of course that Tom Faggus was a gentleman highwayman, forced into his profession by a cruel injustice, and

that he was loyal to the king and truly loved by society and common folk too.

Another relative of our mother's was Reuben Huckaback, as different from Tom Faggus as chalk from cheese. He owned the very best shop in Dulverton town. We being his only kindred, except for his little granddaughter Ruth, Mother kept in touch with him.

When I was still in my teens, but grown huge, this old gentleman informed us that he would be riding our way at Christmas-tide – this being a time when the Doones were lazy and fond of bed. My mother invited our neighbour, Nicholas Snowe, to come in the evening with his three comely daughters to meet Uncle Reuben. And Betty Muxworthy, who did the cooking and kept us all in order with her sharp tongue, was instructed to make a rare good dinner. Because of my great size, she would call me Maister Zider-press, a name which annoyed and ruffled me not a little.

It was thus she greeted me when I came into the kitchen.

"Rackon them Dooneses hath gat him, Maister Ziderpress," she said, when I enquired if Uncle Reuben had arrived.

We waited dinner as long as we could and then ate it before it spoilt. But my mother was on tenterhooks fearing the worst, and at last I set out on foot to look for Uncle Ben.

The fog hung close all around me as I followed the track on to the moor, and my beard, which was now at some length, was full of great drops and prickly. It was a night to make any man tremble in his boots and, presently, I heard through the patter of my own feet a rough low sound which set my heart a-thudding.

Then there came to me through the darkness a long groan, and a choking sound. I made towards the sound and presently was met, point-blank, by the head of a mountain pony. Upon its back lay a man, bound down with his feet on the neck and his head to the tail.

Before the wild little nag could turn, I caught it by its wet and frizzled forelock.

"Fear nothing, no harm shall come to thee," I said to the horse's burden, and

then suddenly exclaimed, "Why, it's Uncle Ben!"

Not to make a long story of it, I cut his bonds and set him astride the nag, but he was too weak to stay there so I carried him on my back, and led the pony by the cords, which I fastened around its nose.

Thanks to my mother's care, it was not long before Master Huckaback recovered both his strength and his spirit. But he was bitter about the Doones, who had robbed him and bound him fast on the wild mountain pony.

Annie and I had not much sympathy for him, for he was the richest man in the county and probably the meanest. But our Eliza gave him all her attention. Her thin little face was eager and glowing when he vowed that he would avenge himself on the murderous thieves.

Lorna steals my heart

I was close on nineteen years old before I paid another visit to Glen Doone, by way of the perilous passage I had discovered in my boyhood.

What drew me back I cannot say. But when I saw Lorna coming towards me among the primroses my heart bounded and I trembled with an emotion I had never before experienced.

She was ready to fly at the unexpected sight of me, but then I fell on the grass and said, "Lorna Doone!"

She knew me at once and a smile came to her sweet lips as she said, laughing, "If you please, who are you, sir, and how do you know my name?"

"I am John Ridd," I answered, "the boy with the fishes . . ."

"Oh, yes, I remember everything," she cried, her large eyes full of a softness and a brightness which made her every word like a poem to me. "But you cannot know, Master Ridd, what the dangers are in this place, and the nature of the people."

"I do know," I said, "and I am greatly frightened – except when I look at you!"

There were to be many further meetings between us but none perhaps as dear and precious as this one, when she stole my heart from me and I became hers forever.

In time she came to tell me her story and of the fear she had of the wild Doones. But she loved her grandfather, Sir Ensor Doone, who, though old and harsh, cherished and protected her. There was no one it seemed she could trust except a little Cornish girl, named Gwenny Carfax, whose life she had saved and who had become her devoted servant and friend.

On my second visit she led me, with many shy and timid glances, towards the upper valley. Here, through the inlet in the rock, was her little bower. It was well concealed, and the opening small, and Lorna laughed quietly as I struggled to follow her, for I was huge compared with her slender shape.

The chamber was of unhewn rock and seemed gay with the rich variety of fern, moss and lichen. Overhead there was no ceiling but the sky itself, and the floor was made of soft, low grass, mixed with moss and wild flowers. Here and there around the sides were chairs of stone, and in the midst a tiny spring of clear water.

This little grotto became our trysting-place. She persuaded me to come only once a month out of fear for my safety, and we arranged a signal. She would cover a white stone, which I could see from a high point on the moors, with her mantle if she felt herself in danger.

One of the Doones I learnt she feared and dreaded more than the others. This was Carver Doone, son of the Counsellor whose father was Sir Ensor, a huge brute of a man who had declared his intention of making her his wife.

My love for Lorna was such that I dreamt of her day and night when we were apart, and my mother was in despair at my loss of appetite. Annie spent all her time in cooking tempting dishes for me, and even sharp-tongued, skinny Eliza sang songs to me to raise my spirits. But although they fussed and bothered about me and would not leave me alone, they did not guess my precious secret.

My steadfast resolve to steal away from our farm to visit Lorna at the end of every month was all at once put to no account by the arrival of an unexpected visitor from London. This was one Jeremy Stickles by name, a King's Messenger.

As I took him into our kitchen, he touched me with a white thing which I saw was a parchment, tied across with cord and fastened down in every corner with unsightly dabs of wax.

"In the name of the King, His Majesty Charles the Second, these presents!" he exclaimed, handing me the scroll.

I broke the seals with a beating heart and saw my own name there. I was required, it seemed, to appear in person before the Right Worshipful the Justices of His Majesty's Bench at Westminster!

A journey to London seemed to us, in those days, as hazardous and dark an adventure as could be forced on any man.

My mother and Annie were all smiles at this summons to Westminster for they thought I would be back in a week as one of His Majesty's great captains. But Jeremy, to whom I took an instant liking, did his best to cheer me up.

We left the next day on horseback and for every moment of that long and weary journey to London my thoughts were with my sweet Lorna.

Of my time in that grand city I will say little. But as the days and then the weeks passed and I was no nearer being summoned, my money began to run out and so too did my patience.

At length, through the good offices of a lawyer who apparently had once known and loved my mother, I found myself being ushered into the presence of the Lord Chief Justice himself.

CAR. I

I will not deny that I was overawed, not only by the chamber itself – which was not very large but was lofty and had wooden panels round it and some raised seats lined with velvet. Three men faced me, wonderfully dressed in fur and robes of state, with curls of long grey horse-hair, crimped and gathered.

The middle one of the three was thick-set and burly, with a blotchy broad face and a great square jaw. He was the Lord Chief Justice Jeffreys, dreaded by all and feared even by the noblemen.

At his invitation I spoke up boldly, telling him that each day I had attended the great hall of Westminster and had not been called to appear and that I was most anxious for permission to return home.

That first interview was brief enough but then there followed another and more intimate interview with no one present in the chamber except Judge Jeffreys. He began to question me closely about the Doones, and the loyalty to the King of the countryfolk in my county. He also mentioned Tom Faggus, whom he admitted he admired but would not be able to save from the gallows should he continue his profession of a Gentleman of the Road.

I gave him straight answers to all his questions and towards the end of our interview he said, "I meant to use thee, Jack, as my tool, but I see that thou art too honest and simple. I will send a sharper fellow, but never let me find thee, John, either a tool for those who would bring about the King's downfall, or a tube for my words to pass through!"

And he gave me such a glare that I longed to be clear of him and of Westminster. But then he suddenly smiled and said in an altered tone of voice, "Now get thee gone, Jack. I shall remember thee!"

A welcome to remember

Two months had passed since I had last set eyes on our farm, and my heart swelled within me as I drew nearer and nearer to the place I loved and owned. Here was the pool where we washed the sheep, and there was the hollow that oozed away, where I had once shot three wild ducks. Here was the peat-rick that hid my dinner when I could not go home for it, and there was the bush with the thyme growing round it where Annie had found a great swarm of our bees. And here was the corner of the dry stone wall marking the end of the moor.

Annie was the first to spy me. She nearly pulled me off my horse, and kissed the mouth of the carbine I was carrying.

"I knew you would come!" she cried, her lovely face all a-glow. "Oh, I may cry now as much as I like for I am so happy!"

Very few can have travelled as far as I had done. And even of those who have done so, not one in a hundred could have had such a warm welcome home. Mother laughed and wept in turns despite her disappointment that I had not been promoted to a great captain by the King. Lizzie watched me silently until I opened my bag and showed her the beautiful present I had for her. It was the best of

all the presents I had, a dear and precious heavy book. I had, too, secreted about my person, a present for my sweet Lorna which I would give to her by and by.

But though I plotted how to leave the farm without being noticed I could not steal away for some days without upsetting my family. And when I did climb to the high spot to gaze away into the distance at the white stone I saw, to my terror, that it was covered by Lorna's cloak. She had sent me the danger signal and I had not been there to answer it!

Nothing now could stop me going to her. When at last I stood in the niche of rock at the head of the slippery waterfall and gazed into the quiet glen, I could only pray that somehow she would know I was there and would come to me.

And come she did. I went slowly towards her, and said all I could say in the first moment.

"Mistress Lorna, I had hoped that you were in need of me."

"Oh yes," said she, "but that was long ago, two months ago or more, sir."

I was so dazed and frightened at her words and the way she would not meet my eyes that I gave out a stupid sob. Hearing it, Lorna took pity on me and held out both her hands to me. Then she led me into her secret bower and I told her of my summons to London and all that kept me from her. Lorna told me in her turn that the brutal Carver Doone had once again tried to make her promise to be his wife.

"Even my grandfather has tried to make me swear a solemn oath to marry him – even though he is at least twice my age," she finished sadly.

I scowled ferociously at her words but was even more alarmed when she went on to tell me that she was now guarded most closely and that if it hadn't been for the cunning of her loyal little serving girl, Gwenny Carfax, she would not have been able to come to the bower.

She looked so lovely, with her dark eyelashes trembling, and her soft eyes full of light, that I could only whisper, "Dearest, love of my life!"

And then I took from my pocket the ring of sapphire and pearls which I had bought for her in London and slipped it on her finger.

I knew from the sudden light of happiness in her eyes and her quick blushes and the music in her voice as she thanked me for my gift that she had now begun to love me, and my heart leapt for joy.

On my return to the farm I found it hard to keep a sober face and was conscious that a change too had come over my favourite sister. I noted that whenever Tom Faggus's name was mentioned she blushed as prettily as my Lorna had done.

When we found ourselves alone, I asked Annie straight out if she meant to marry him. From her shining eyes I knew what the answer would be when the time was ripe. She in her turn amazed me by talking of the Doones and asking me what took me abroad so often.

"Can your love cook as well as me?" she asked suddenly, taking me off my guard.

"No, of course not!" I answered rashly. "She is not a mere cook – why Lorna Doone is . . ."

"Oh, Lorna Doone, Lorna Doone!" exclaimed Annie, clapping her hands with triumph. "Lorna Doone has stolen my brother's heart!"

Now Annie shared my secret and I shared hers. We both knew, however, that sooner or later our dear mother must be told. There was no doubt she would be greatly vexed that I had given my heart to a Doone maid. But I felt that if once I could get her to meet Lorna, she would love her on sight.

When I was pondering how best I could break the news to her of my engagement, Tom Faggus came on his strawberry mare, Winnie, and was at once invited indoors to share our meal. I noticed that there was something odd about his manner. He seemed sober and nervous, though he cast soft, sly looks at Annie.

I asked him to come with me to see the ploughing but he refused and I went off alone, knowing that he meant to talk to my mother. When I returned, Tom Faggus was gone, and my mother was in tears.

"Oh, John, speak one good word for us," Annie pleaded, taking my hand.

"Not one, but a hundred," I said. "Come, Mother, let us go into the garden and sit upon the bench, for I too have

something very important to tell you."

We sat there quietly until I could find the words to tell my mother of Lorna and my love for her. And when at last they came and she knew how it was between us, she took it all most calmly.

Uppermost in her mind was the danger I ran each time I visited my sweetheart, and she began to make plans for fetching Lorna, in some wonderful manner, out of the power of the Doones.

November came and I had seen Lorna but once in two months, but what happiness it was to tell her of my mother's plans, and to assure her that her true home was now Plover's Barrows farm.

I wore now the ring my love had given me at our last meeting. It was a broad, very ancient thumb ring with a worn crest upon it, which she told me had been attached to a childhood glass necklace. I mention this ring particularly because it plays a part in the history of my Lorna.

In that month of November, Jeremy Stickles came to see us, and by his secretive manner and evasive answers I knew there was some mischief afoot.

"Stick to the winning side, John," was all he would say.

"That is the very thing I want to do, for the sake of Lorna – that is to say, for the sake of my dear mother and sisters, and the farm."

"Ha!" cried Jeremy, laughing at the redness of my face. "Lorna, saidst thou? Now what Lorna?"

"Mind your own business," I answered, very proudly, "and spy as much as you like but not into my affairs."

I was so roused that I left him, and went to work at the sacks on the cornfloor.

But now my own affairs were thrown into disorder and Lorna herself was the cause of it. Three times I went and waited at the bottom of the valley for a sight of her and she did not come. Once I even went far up the valley within a stone's throw of the last outlying hut. This was a gloomy, low square house, without any light in the windows, roughly built of wood and stone. I guessed that it was Carver Doone's dwelling, and when I saw that it was empty, I surveyed it carefully.

Before I took myself home that night, I had resolved to penetrate Glen Doone from the upper end, and try to find my beloved Lorna.

In search of Lorna

To venture into the very stronghold of the Doones was, I knew, an act of madness, but all the same I set out the very next night. I went on foot, as I did not dare take a horse for fear that the Doones might be abroad on their usual business.

When at length I came upon the robbers' track I followed it warily until I drew near to the entrance to their stronghold. Across the three rude, overhanging archways into their township was suspended a felled oak, black and thick and threatening. This, as I had heard before, could be dropped in a moment to crush the enemy. But now I must choose the entrance which would lead me into the valley. Rumour had it that if I chose the wrong one I would presently be plunged into the bottomless depths of water and seen no more.

After some hesitation I chose the middle one and, grasping my long ash staff, tipped with iron, I groped my way along the rocky wall in black darkness.

Towards the end of that long twisting tunnel I almost stumbled over two sentries, both huge men. They were engaged in some trivial game of push-pin and were smoking long clay pipes. I drew back in alarm and pressed myself against the rock face. I would surely have been discovered if they had not begun quarrelling over the game. The younger of the two men – a handsome, merry fellow whom I knew to be one Charlie Doone – was more than a little drunk, and presently he flung the contents of his glass in his comrade's face. It missed and hit the open lantern which spluttered and went out. In the gloom I slipped past them and round the corner.

"Curse it, Charlie," grumbled his friend, "now you'll have to go down to Carver and get a new wick."

As Charlie stood up and reeled away I slipped after him.

Down a steep and winding path, with a handrail at the corners, Charlie tripped until he reached the top of the meadow land, with its bubbling little stream. From there I had a view of the robbers' township, for the moon was out.

Master Charlie went down the village, and I followed him carefully, keeping as much as possible to the shadowy places. But as I passed Sir Ensor's house, which I recognized from Lorna's description, my heart leaped, for I spied a barred window faintly lit. As I stared up at it, Lorna herself came to the window.

"Oh, Lorna, don't you know me?" I whispered, showing myself.

"Are you mad?" she answered immediately. "Go away, John, and never think of me again. All is over between us."

And she put her little hand through the

cruel bars. I grasped it and begged her to tell me why she had given me no sign or signal these past months.

"My poor grandfather is very ill," she said, with a sob, "and the Counsellor and his son are now the masters of the valley. Carver seized me when I tried to go out and signal to you. Once my poor grandfather dies I am at their mercy. You must go back. I shall die if they catch you . . ."

But I would not budge and presently Gwenny Carfax, Lorna's little servant girl, came to the window and was introduced to me.

"Whoy!" cried Gwenny, in great amazement, "Her be bigger nor any Doone! I shall knoo thee again, young man, no fear of that."

"She is the best in the world," said Lorna, when the little maid had gone. "And if only you will go I promise you shall hear when I am in danger."

"But how?" I urged. "How?"

"Gwenny can climb like a cat," Lorna said, in the same soft, clear voice. "You see that tree with the seven rooks' nests, bright against the cliffs there? Can you count them from above, do you think?"

"Surely, surely!" I exclaimed. "Perhaps from our copse."

"Gwenny has climbed that tree many times in the summer. Now the nests are empty. She will take one away if I am in peril and want you. If you see but five I am carried off by Carver!"

I cried out then in a voice of such misery and horror that she drew back.

"Fear not, John," she whispered sadly. "I have the means to stop him. He shall not take me alive."

What could I say then but, "God bless you, my darling," before stealing away and taking my well-known secret track out of that dark and terrible valley.

All through the days and nights that followed my desperate venture into Doone valley my thoughts were with Lorna. But I could still take a share in Annie's happiness when, one morning, Tom Faggus came riding by on his sweet mare, Winnie, to tell us that he had been granted the King's Pardon and had purchased a piece of land. So my sister's highwayman was now a respectable landowner, and we were pleased for both their sakes.

To the copse of young ash I went every afternoon. From there I had a clear view of the tree which held the seven rooks' nests, and so long as all seven were visible I did not worry so much. I worked hard in that copse with my bill-hook and shearing knife, cutting out the saplings and making spars to keep for thatching.

And now a thing came to pass which tested my love for Lorna to its limit. I would far rather have faced Carver Doone and his father than have met, in cold blood, Sir Ensor Doone, the founder of the colony and the fear of the fiercest.

It happened in this manner. I went up one morning early to look for my seven rooks' nests, unwilling for some reason to delay until later – and, though I rubbed my eyes and looked and looked, I could count only six. To enter Doone valley in

broad daylight would be to court certain death, and I ran to the nearest place where I could remain unseen, and watched the glen for hours and hours.

When it was growing dark, I was just about to make a circle of the hills when suddenly, out of the thickly wooded hollow to my left, came Gwenny Carfax.

"Young man," she said, "you must come with me. Old man be dying, and he can't die, or at least won't, without first considering thee."

"What can Sir Ensor Doone want with me?" I asked in amazement. "Has Mistress Lorna told him about me?"

Whereupon Gwenny nodded, saying, "All concerning thee is known."

I burned and shivered at the very idea of facing that dreaded tyrant, but I nevertheless sent Watch, my sheepdog, home and followed Gwenny. The night was icy cold but I thought nothing of my discomfort as Gwenny glided before me. She led me into Doone valley, and then forward to Sir Ensor's door.

Lorna opened it herself and drew me inside. She took me into a cold dark room where an old man, very stern and handsome, sat upright in a chair, his loose red cloak thrown over him. His white hair fell upon his shoulders, and his pale hands lay lifelessly on his lap.

I saw death in his face and was at a loss for words. But presently he spoke, as Lorna left the room.

"Are you the great John Ridd?" he asked.

"Yes," said I.

"Then hearken to me, boy: I forbid you ever to see that foolish child again. You will pledge your word in Lorna's presence never to see or to seek her again. Now call her back, for I am weary . . ."

I found her in the next room crying softly to herself, and without a word I led her to her grandfather. We stood there before him, hand in hand.

"Ye two fools!" the old man said at last.

Whereupon Lorna, with shining eyes,

reached up and kissed me.

"Fools you are and fools you'll be forever," went on Sir Ensor Doone. "The best I can wish you is that you be boy and girl to each other until the grandchildren come . . ."

Some time later the old man died, and only Lorna and I were with him as he lay very still and quiet in his bed. But in his last moments he looked at us both very gently as if he wished to do something for us. On seeing how he let his hand drop downward, I whispered, "He wants something out of the bed, dear." Lorna bade me grope among the pillows.

There I felt something hard and sharp and drew it out and gave it to him. It flashed, like the spray of a fountain upon us, in the dark winter of the room. He could not take it in his poor, shrunken hand, but somehow made Lorna see that he meant her to have it.

"Why, it is my glass necklace!" Lorna cried. "My necklace he promised me, and from which you have got the ring, John."

And she began to weep as the old man gave a single, feeble nod to show that he understood. Then his spirit left him.

No one wept for the passing of the ancient outlaw except his granddaughter, my beloved Lorna. When something of her grief was passed I swore that I would return and take her from the robbers' village before Carver could have his way.

A winter to remember

The night after I returned home, there came such a storm of snow the like of which no man in our parts had ever before witnessed.

It snowed without ceasing for close on eight hours, and our sheep were buried in it and numbers of them lost. We worked all the next day like madmen to save as many of them as we were able, in blizzards which threatened to bury men as well as beasts.

And after the snow came the frost, such a frost that froze our very kettle by the fire and the soup in the pan. Some of our men died from it, and the cattle were frozen stiff in their head-ropes.

I grew frantic with impatience to go to Lorna and yet could not because of the drifts of frozen snow. In the end, Lizzie, our little bookworm, told me how she had

once read in a book concerning the Arctic that men walked over the frozen wastes in snow-shoes.

"They are not hard to make, John," she said. "If you will listen I'll read you what my book says . . ."

I set to work, with Lizzie as my instructor, and soon I had built myself a pair of strong and light snow-shoes as good as any, I warrant, that could be found in the Arctic regions.

At first I was not able to walk in them, but I practised diligently until I could move over the snow quite fast. When I had done as much as a man could do about the farm, I told my mother that I meant to go and fetch Lorna home, and that she must keep the fires blazing until my return.

Then I got out our new light pony-sled, which I must pull myself, and loaded it up with provisions and two or three fur coats.

The moon rose like a bright silver penny as I set out over the hard-packed snow. Not daring to risk an avalanche from the cliff-tops, I chose to make my way through the narrow chasm towards the whirlpool and the waterfall – the very route I had once taken in my boyhood days. And lo, the fall was solid ice!

Leaving the sled moored at the very lip of the chasm, I set off up the valley, skirting along one side of it. All the Doones were safely inside their dwellings on such a night and I reached Lorna's house unnoticed.

If I live to be a hundred, I shall not forget the scene that met my eyes as I entered the house and saw Lorna crouched in a corner behind a chair, with a man towering over her and trying to draw the chair away. Another of the Doones stood over little Gwenny, who had him fast by the ankle. In a moment I had sent the first crashing through the window, and the second through the door into the snowdrift.

Then I caught up Lorna in my arms and, bidding Gwenny follow us, I bore my sweet burden to the sled, and wrapped her in one of the great fur coats. Unpursued, yet forever looking back, we made a perilous descent down the slippery ice-

slope. Then, skirting the black whirlpool, we gained the meadows beyond it.

What can I write of Lorna's home-coming, beyond saying that in the first few moments of setting her down in our warm kitchen she had captured my mother's heart!

In the days and weeks that followed, Lorna was so loved, even adored, by all who got to know her, that I had it in my heart to be jealous. But then she would look at me with such love and devotion in her large soft eyes, that I knew she was mine for eternity.

We kept a strict watch now all around the farm, for we knew that an attack from the Doones was almost certain to come. But the vast drifts of snow, some fifty feet high, kept the Doones in their valley. The

snow and frost, we knew, could not last forever, and when after three months the rain came down on us, from a south-west wind, we were faced with another threat to our livelihood – that of flooding.

It was now high time to work very hard, both to make up for the farm-work lost during the snow blizzards, and also to prepare ourselves for a great and vicious attack from the Doones, who would burn us in our beds at the earliest opportunity.

One of our first callers at the end of that memorable winter was Tom Faggus, and though much of his attention was for our sweet Annie, he was loud in his praise of my Lorna's grace and beauty.

After she had left us one night, and we were seated round the fire, he remarked, "The Doones will never let her go." Then he continued, a grave note of warning in his voice, "and all the more so because of that necklace she wears!"

"What!" I cried. "That common glass thing which she has had from her childhood?"

"Glass indeed!" exclaimed Tom. "They are the finest brilliants ever I set eyes on. Why – if I were not reformed . . ." And here he glanced at my mother, who had joined us. ". . . I would stop an eight-horse coach with armed outriders for such booty . . ."

Seeing my look of huge disbelief, my mother went to Lorna, telling her to come down among us again, with the necklace. As she entered the room, she took the necklace and sweetly and graciously

handed it to my mother.

"A hundred thousand pounds at least!" exclaimed Tom, taking it from my mother. "These diamonds and brilliants cannot be matched in London."

"Dear mother, I am so glad," Lorna said softly, when she had got over her astonishment. "You will have it, won't you, as a gift from me . . .?"

I was so overcome by her generous gesture that I scarcely paid close attention to what Tom was saying next – that the necklace could only have come from the very highest, the noblest family in England.

Tom Faggus took his departure the next day, having spoken to my mother about a date for marrying our Annie. Scarcely had his high-stepping mare taken him out of sight, than in came Master Jeremy Stickles, splashed with mud from head to foot, and not in the best of tempers.

Part of his commission, it seemed, was to organize the defeat of the Doones, and to discover any among us county folk who were rebels, and secretly plotting to bring about the downfall of King Charles. Jeremy had mounted troopers stationed at Lynmouth, and fearing that our farm would be soon under attack, he asked me to ride there and fetch them back while he went off in search of equipment.

It was while we were both away that the Counsellor, Carver Doone's father, dared to come to our house. So pleasant was he, and so gracious and affectionate towards my Lorna, that both mother and Annie were taken in by him and invited him to stay the night.

Annie, especially, took a liking to the silver-haired old man – especially when he condemned all those who spoke against Tom Faggus.

Thus it came about that the sly, soft-spoken old villain bemused her with some silly old wives' tale the next morning, as he followed her into the dairy to watch her making clotted cream.

"Have you ever heard," asked the Counsellor, "that if you pass a string of beads of polished glass across the top of

the cream pan, breaking the surface, the cream will set three times as solid, and in thrice the quantity?"

"No, sir, I had not heard that," said Annie, staring at him with her simple eyes. "But I will fetch my coral necklace and we can try."

"No, no, not coral, my child," said the Counsellor quickly. "The beads must be shining – the brighter the better."

"Then I know the very thing!" Annie cried. "Lorna's necklace! It is the very thing!"

"Then fetch it at once," said the old man. "And remember, what we do must be done in secret or else the charm will not work and the cream will fail to clot."

So Annie, trusting the old villain, ran to Lorna's room and took the necklace out of its secret-hole near the head of Lorna's bed and ran down with it to the dairy.

"Oh, that old thing!" exclaimed the Counsellor contemptuously, taking the necklace, and passing it over the pan, at the same time muttering, "Crinklemm, crankum, grass and clover!" The words so scared Annie that she grew quite terrified as she stood there.

"Now, child," said he, after a pause. "Put the bauble under the pannikin and, so that the spell may work and no harm come to you, go in secret to your room, bolt yourself in for three hours and read the Lord's Prayer backwards . . ."

Poor simple Annie! When she returned to the dairy, the black-hearted rascal was

gone and so too was the priceless necklace!

On hearing the sad story of the stolen necklace, I would have scolded Annie soundly if it had not been for Lorna's gentle insistence that we were all better off without it. And indeed Annie's pretty eyes were so red with weeping over her folly that we grew sorry for her and had not the heart to upbraid her.

That night, when Jeremy Stickles was with us once again, and we found ourselves alone in the parlour, I told him the full story of the necklace, and showed him the ring, which had been on the front of it.

"I, too, have a story to tell you, John," he said, taking out his pipe. And he told me that, while he was riding from Dulverton to Watchett, he had come upon a lonely inn just before dusk and had determined to spend the night there.

"The landlady was an Italian, Benita by name," he went on, "and married to an Englishman. We fell into conversation and she told me how she came to be in that desolate spot."

"Go on," I said impatiently. "What have your Italian landlady and that lonely inn to do with our affairs?"

"Benita had once been a lady's maid to a noble English family, the noblest in the land," Jeremy said slowly. "The young lord was tragically killed while the family was in Italy. And the beautiful young widow with her two children, a boy and a girl, decided to return to these parts – taking Benita with them . . ."

I felt my heart beat faster as memory took me back to a steep hill and a great coach labouring up it, but I held my tongue, as Jeremy took up his story once more.

"Well, after leaving Dulverton town, the fog came down, and their grand coach was set upon by the lawless Doones. The postilions drove the horses into the sea, but before the waves came into the coach, a score of desperate men were around it. Both the fine lady and the boy were drowned, but not the girl child . . ."

"What became of her – the girl?" I cried in an agony of suspense.

"Carried off by the Doones," said Jeremy, sucking at his empty pipe, "and according to Benita, the little maid had the diamond necklace round her neck. Benita put it there herself, concealing it under the child's travelling cloak . . ."

"And – and this Benita?" I asked, as I recalled in a sudden flash the foreign lady I had met in my schoolboy days.

"Ah yes, apparently she was stunned by a blow on the head and left on the shore," answered Jeremy. "She was found the next morning, and, with no hope of ever returning to her own country, she settled in these parts and eventually married the landlord of the inn."

I buried my face in my hands to hide the depth of feeling Jeremy's story had aroused in me. Then I asked, "Who was that little girl? Who do you think she was?"

And Jeremy answered without hesitation, "Why, as certain as I sit here, that little maid is Lorna Doone!"

A battle fought and lost

In the months that followed many events took place which I shall relate but briefly.

Jeremy Stickles lodged his troopers in our barns until the moment was ripe for the attack on the Doone stronghold. When that moment came, we were joined by a number of stalwarts from Devon and Somerset. Then "Colonel Stickles", as we now called him, drew up his plan of campaign.

Alas for our high hopes of winning the battle and wiping out the lawless Doones forever! As some of us, led by Jeremy, advanced among the crags, we were suddenly under fire from the robbers, who were hidden overhead in the gallery of brushwood. We leapt in under the very feet of our enemy, but when the foremost among us were past the entrance to their village, an awful crash sounded behind us, with the shrieks of men, the din of metal and the horrible screaming of horses.

The trunk of the huge tree had been launched overhead, and crashed into the very midst of us. Our cannon was under it, and so were two men, and a horse with its poor back broken. As another horse vainly struggled to rise, I lost all presence of mind, for I loved both those good horses. Shouting for any to follow me, I dashed headlong into the cavern.

Some five or six men came after me, the

foremost of whom was Jeremy. I leapt forward down that tunnel like a madman and, pouncing upon one of the gunners, flung him across his own cannon. But the others fled, and a heavy oak door closed with a bang behind them. With all my remaining strength I caught up the Doone cannon with both hands and dashed it, breech-first, at the doorway. The solid oak burst with the blow, and the gun stuck fast.

But now I looked round in vain for others to come and support me. No figures moved through the length of the tunnel behind me, and I hurried back to find two already dead, and Jeremy sorely wounded with his poor face shattered.

The battle continued then in a half-hearted manner until it became clear the Doones had the better of us, and that our losses were too serious for us to fight on.

Our defeat was all the more shameful when it became known that only some thirty Doones had succeeded in routing hundreds of troopers and other fighting men. And, though we nursed Jeremy back to health, he was never again the same man.

Meanwhile I had other matters of the greatest importance on my mind. Lorna

was gone from Plover's Barrows – gone to London to lay claim to her noble father's vast fortune. It was no more than I expected after taking her to that lonely inn to meet Benita. There was too, the evidence of the ancient ring which was recognized as a family heirloom.

Annie was gone as well, Tom Faggus having married her and set her up in a house of her own. It grieved me in many ways that she should have given herself so gladly to a highwayman, even though he was a reformed one!

We all missed Annie sorely for, with the best will in the world, our little Lizzie could not take her place in the kitchen, and our meals were far from appetizing.

But it was not Lizzie's poor fare that drove the colour from my cheeks and brought new furrows to my brow. Months passed, and I wrote many letters to my Lady Lorna, and never a one came back from her.

We had no doubt that she was alive and well for, time and again, reports reached our farm of the wealth and beauty of young Lady Lorna Dugal, who had become a favourite at court, and among the common people.

As if my sweetheart's strange silence was not enough to worry and puzzle me – there came other news that alarmed us all. We heard it first in church, on a Sunday in February, and so startled were we that we were all thrown into a panic. King Charles the Second was dead!

There followed then rumours of disturbances and plottings, and of movements of troops about the country – and through it all we expected the Doones to attack the farm and finish us off. But still we continued to plough the land and tend the cattle and wish for quieter and more settled times.

There came a day in July, however, when I returned from the mowing to find

a little cart, such as high-born folk use, in our courtyard. On entering the kitchen, there was our Annie, with her baby son in her arms, looking pale and tearful.

At the sight of me she burst into sobs. When at last I could make sense of what she was saying, it was to learn that Tom had gone off with the rebels, and that she wanted me to go after him and fetch him home.

I could not hold out against Annie's wishes for long, although my mother was angry that she should be the means of sending me off on such a dangerous venture. And so, early one morning, I saddled my good Kickums who, although he had but one sound eye and a mean nature, was worth ten sweet-tempered horses to a man who knew how to manage him.

I took with me a little kettle, a pound and a half of tobacco, three pipes, bread and meat, and a change of clothing, and considered myself well equipped for a long campaign. It was likely that the rebels would be moving from place to place, though I had no idea where King Monmouth's army would be So when I came close to Dulverton town, I turned off the road and made for Master Huckaback's house in the hopes that Uncle Reuben would give me a bite to eat.

To my surprise, the old man was away from home. It was left to Ruth, his granddaughter and now grown into an attractive young woman, to tend to my needs and give me all the news.

She looked so worried and concerned at

the news of my enterprise that I began to wonder if she had a deeper feeling than mere affection for me. But I said nothing, and she wished me God-speed after feeding me most handsomely.

For some time I rode on, my course being dictated by rumours of engagements between the rebels and the King's soldiers, and my hopes of ever finding Tom Faggus alive or dead grew fainter with every passing day.

One morning, guided by the sound of guns and trumpets, we came upon a broad open moor where, to my horror, I saw young men lying, some wounded, others dead. The sight was so terrible that it has stayed with me all my days.

I got down from Kickums and knelt by a youth whose life was ebbing away. While I tried to persuade him to drink from my flask, I felt warm lips laid against my cheek quite softly, and then a little push, and behold it was a horse leaning over

me! I got up quickly and there stood Winnie! She looked at me with beseeching eyes, enough to melt a heart of stone. If ever a horse tried hard to speak, it was Winnie and I knew what she was trying to tell me and what she wanted me to do.

She waited while I finished tending the dying soldier, then I mounted Kickums and went after her over that battle-scarred moor.

The faithful creature, whom I began to love as if she were my own, stopped at last in front of a low black shed. Here she uttered a little greeting, in a subdued and softened voice, hoping to obtain an answer from her beloved master.

Receiving no signal, she entered, and I leapt off Kickums's back, and followed. Tom Faggus was there all right but to my eyes he looked already dead. Winnie, however, reached out her long slender neck and touched him, as gentle as a woman, with her under lip. Then she looked up at me again as if to tell me that I could not let him die.

At death's door Tom might have been, but when I gave him what aid I could, and he was able to open his eyes and see, standing there, his beautiful mare, new strength seemed to flow into his limbs.

"Pull me upright, Jack," he whispered, and when I got him into a sitting position, he asked, "Is Winnie hurt?"

"She is sound as a bell," I replied.

"Then so am I," he said. "Now bind me up and set me upon her back. She'll take me home."

And when I had done this, with many a scared look at his ashen face, I set him in the saddle and bound him to it.

Then Tom sucked his lips, and the mare took him outside and carried him off, as swift and easy as a swallow.

Gwenny's treachery

I will now pass lightly over my encounter with the King's forces and how my good friend, Jeremy Stickles, saved me from being shot as a rebel. Through his good offices, and taking his advice which was always sound, I set my face for London.

To meet and talk with Lorna was now the only purpose I had in life. To this end I found rooms with an old furrier until I could discover where she lived.

I found out at last that she was in the house of a nobleman, Earl Brandir, and to this magnificent dwelling I went one Sunday evening, going round to the servants' entrance rather than to the main door. To my surprise, who should come and let me in but little Gwenny Carfax! I was so pleased to see her that I tried to give her a friendly kiss, but she turned her face away and looked ashamed.

She showed me into a little room, very daintily furnished and left me without a word. Almost before I had begun to hope that I would find Lorna as true to me as I had been to her, the crimson velvet hangings of the doorway parted, and there she stood in all her perfect beauty. Her dress was pure white, but her face as she looked at me was a blushing rosy pink.

I took the hand she offered me and gently kissed it and then, in another instant, she was weeping at my breast.

Oh, how wonderfully the time passed as we clung to each other. And then came the moment for exchanging stories and for explanations.

"Why, oh why, did you send me no message?" she asked plaintively.

"And why did you send me none?" I answered. "Not a single reply to any of my letters!"

"What!" cried Lorna. "But I sent you many and wondered at your silence."

We stared at each other, amazed, until Lorna summoned her little maid. Gwenny came at once and we both knew from her sullen and guilty air that it was she who had stolen our letters.

"Did you think it was honest to do such a thing?" Lorna asked her sadly, and the fiery Cornish girl burst into a storm of weeping, crying that she had only wanted to stop her lady from marrying a poor common farming chap!

Gwenny's treachery had cost us both dear, but Lorna was still mine. In the days that followed I was accepted by Lord Brandir, who was as kind and noble an old gentleman as you could hope to meet.

Chance put me in the way of doing him a great service, when I saved him from the attentions of some rogues who broke into his house. As a consequence of this and some of my previous exploits against the Doones, I found myself one day in the presence of His Majesty!

"I am well pleased with thee, John Ridd," says he. "Thou hast done great service to the realm, and to religion . . ."

"So this is the great Johann Reed!" cries Her Majesty, coming forward. "I have heard much of him from the dear, dear Lorna."

"Well," says His Majesty, all of a sudden, "what is thy chief ambition, lad?"

I thought for a moment and then remembering my mother's firm belief that I was worthy of a coat of arms, I told the King that that was what I wanted.

"Thou shalt have it, lad," said he, smiling. He motioned me to kneel, which I did, and then he gave me a little tap very nicely upon my shoulder before I knew what he was about, and said, "Arise, Sir John Ridd!"

This so astonished me that all I could find to say was, "Sir, I am very much obliged. But what be I to do with it?"

As for the coat of arms devised for me, it delighted my mother beyond speech, for it was of great size and very colourful.

With Lorna's promise that we should be wed as soon as she was able to settle her affairs in London, I returned to the farm – only to learn that the Doones, with Captain Carver at their head, had robbed and pillaged many of the smaller places, and were now the terror of two counties.

Tom Faggus, whose faithful mare had borne him safely home as he had said she would, was now fully recovered. Very anxious he was to join the great band of men willing to march against the Doones, and make an end of their stronghold once and for all.

Suffice to say, I became their leader, and we contrived to trick and surprise them, and so gain entry into their village. We burnt their houses and, apart from the women and children, scarcely left a Doone alive. I had the privilege of cornering the old, silver-haired Counsellor and taking from him Lorna's necklace. But I let him go free, knowing that we would never see him again.

Alas, Carver Doone, the most desperate villain of them all, avoided capture. He set his great black horse at Doone-gate at full gallop, and our yeomen fell back and let him through. I could not blame them but to know that he was at large and furious was no light matter. In his flight he left behind his little boy, Ensie, who took a liking to me and I to him, and we cared for him at the farm.

But now news came from London that Lorna would soon be with us. When at last she came, it seemed as if the whole house was full of a brightness – it was as if the sun had come over the hill, and my Lorna was his looking-glass. My mother sat in an ancient chair, and wiped her cheeks and gazed at her, I ran outside like a madman and flung my best hat on the barn, and kissed old Mother Fry till she shooed me off with her wooden spoon.

Before the date of our wedding was fixed, the high and mighty Lord Chancellor Jeffreys came to our farm of his own accord to give Lorna, who was his ward, permission, under sign and seal, to marry "that loyal knight, John Ridd, upon condition only that the King's consent should be obtained".

We had no thought that this would be withheld, and when it came we fixed our wedding day without any fear of a hitch. We heard then that people meant to come

from more than thirty miles around, partly to see my great stature (for I was famous for my wrestling) and partly to see Lorna's beauty.

All the ins and outs of our wedding day were arranged by my mother. When at last it came, I scarcely knew where to place my feet for the sweeping dresses worn by Lizzie and all the females from our neighbouring farms. Even pretty Ruth Huckaback had come, though Mother said she had needed a great deal of persuading, and perhaps, in my heart, I knew why.

When Lorna came out of a pew half-way down our church she took my left hand in her right, and she looked so beautiful in her dress of purest white, clouded with faint lavender, that I grew afraid almost to glance her way, except of course when I placed the ring upon her slender finger.

It is impossible for any, who have not loved as I have, to imagine my joy and pride, as Lorna turned to look at me. And as her loving eyes met mine – the sound of a shot rang through the church, and Lorna fell across my knees just when I was about to kiss her. Her blood stained the yellow wood of the altar steps, as I lifted her up, and petted her, begging her, beseeching her to live. She sighed a long sigh on my breast, and then she grew so cold, so very cold that I asked what time of year it could be.

An end and a beginning

I knew, of course, who had robbed me of my sweet Lorna and, laying my wife in my mother's arms, I left the church.

Just as I was, and with her blood upon my wedding suit, I leapt upon our best horse, with bridle but no saddle, and set the head of Kickums in the direction the men pointed out to me. Riding at furious speed I came upon Black Barrow Down, and there, about a furlong before me, rode a man on a great black horse. I knew that the man was Carver Doone.

"Thy life or mine," I said to myself, and urged Kickums on.

Over that long moor I followed him, and I saw now that he had something set before him, little Ensie, his son. He looked back only once before he turned up the gully that leads from the moor to a rocky chasm and a bottomless swamp.

I followed my enemy carefully, steadily, for I had him, as in a pitfall, from which no escape was possible. Rising from my horse's back, I caught hold of a gnarled and half-starved oak that hung from a crag above me.

Carver Doone turned the corner suddenly, and came upon the black and fearful bog. With a start of fear he reined back his horse, but then rode on, hoping to find a way round the side. Then all at once he wheeled round, fired and rode at me. His bullet struck me somewhere but I took no notice and, with the limb of the oak, struck him full on the forehead. He fell from his horse, and I too leapt on to the ground. The little boy ran to me, and I told him to run round the corner and try to find some bluebells for the pretty lady.

Then I was ready to meet my enemy, and he came at me with a sullen and black scowl. I think he knew by the way I stood and the look in my blue eyes that

he had met his master at last.

At any rate an ashy paleness came into his cheeks, and the vast calves of his legs bowed in, as if he were out of training. He caught me round the waist with a grip that I would not have believed possible, and I heard my ribs crack. But then I grasped his arm and took him by the throat. In two minutes I had him helpless. Even so, I could not make an end of him in cold blood.

But before I could give him the chance to recover, the black bog had him by the feet. The sucking ground drew him on and downwards, and I myself had scarcely time to leap from that dreaded grave of slime. I could not help him but could only stare and gasp as slowly he vanished before my eyes. Then his little boy came back with the bluebells, and I gathered him up in my arms and placed him upon my horse.

It was lucky for me that Kickums went home as mildly as a lamb or else I would have fallen from the saddle. As it was, when we reached our farmhouse, I was only able to totter inside before collapsing.

"I killed him," I gasped, "just as he killed my Lorna!" And then my senses left me.

On recovering consciousness, I was so overwhelmed with grief at the loss of my dearest wife that I would most willingly have died and though Annie nursed me with a devotion which was typical of her love, I yet grew weaker and could not even get downstairs.

One afternoon a gentle knock sounded through my gloomy room, and to my surprise little Ruth came in. She was gaily dressed and I felt sorry for her bad taste, thinking she had come to bewitch and conquer me, now that Lorna was gone.

"Can you receive visitors, Cousin Ridd?" she asked me, smiling. Then she stopped short at the sight of my poor thin face. "But what has the doctor been doing to you? How ill and weak you look."

I had no need to tell her, for the basin by my chair told her that part of my treatment was blood-letting.

"This blood-letting has all but killed

you!" she suddenly cried, and with her little foot she crushed the basin. "From now on I shall take care of you and nurse you back to health as I have done for Lorna."

"Lorna!" I said feebly. "You have saved my Lorna's life? What do you mean by talking so?"

"Only what I say, Cousin John. None would believe that I had skill enough to save her, but save her I did . . ."

"I do not understand," I whispered.

"Will you understand if I show you Lorna?" she asked. "We feared for your reason since you believed so strongly that she was dead. That is why we have kept her from you – but now, well you shall see . . ."

She left me then but presently came back, and behind her, Lorna, hanging back as if shy. All at once, Ruth turned and banged the door behind her and we were alone.

At the risk of all my thick bandages and upsetting the dozen medicine bottles, and scattering leeches right and left, she managed to get into my arms, although they were too weak to hold her.

I felt my life come back to me then, and the joy of living and of loving. How long we stayed there together I cannot tell. But my gloomy room was transformed into a place of light and happiness.

There is now not much more I have to tell. Lorna never tired of sitting and watching me eat and eat until I grew strong again and was able to manage our farm.

And although she has a great store of money, she delights in simple things and loves nothing better than being a farmer's wife – and mother to our children.

Thanks to Jeremy Stickles, Tom and Annie are leading good and respectable lives, and Tom still has his wonderful horse, Winnie, to carry him over the moors.

Lizzie finally put all her books on the shelf and vowed she would marry a certain Captain who came to our farm in the troubled times. This delighted our mother, who still loves to have a hand in weddings.

I sent little Ensie to my old school at Tiverton at my own cost, having changed his name for fear of what anyone might do to him if it became known that his father was the dreaded Carver Doone.

Ruth Huckaback is not yet married, but on her grandfather's death she was very well provided for, and I know a certain worthy man who loves her truly, and who may one day find her willing to be his wife.

As for Lorna, my lifelong darling – year by year her beauty grows with the growth of goodness, kindness and true happiness. And if sometimes she teases me and I, in my turn, wish to quieten her high spirits and call to mind all the sad and joyous times we have been through together, I have but to whisper the two magical words, "Lorna Doone".